Chapter 1: Close Enough

After waking up in a cold sweat, I struggle to open my eyes because I feel like I have just run a marathon. I sigh and then raise my hand to wipe the crusts off my eyelids for merely a second before I drop my left hand to the bed beside me. The moment I do, I notice that the black silky sheets under my fingertips seem to be wet with something warm, so I glance down. When I see it, I stare blankly at the dark red puddle staining the fabric. However, when I move my hand to the side quickly, I feel an object squish underneath the sheet.

Right away, I wonder how I could have been so stupid while climbing out of bed as quickly as I can. In the meantime, I almost trip while wiping my hand on my red silky nightgown in disgust. After all, it is stained with the same dark red substance, and I already know what has happened. The exact same thing that happens every time.

The first time I remember waking up with blood on my hands, was the morning of my 11th birthday. I had a visitor in my room the night before, like every night before that one. It was a common occurrence for me, and I had come to realize that it always would. That is unless someone stopped him from doing it.

At age 11, my other had decided enough was enough. She had taken over every time he snuck into my room at night. I thanked God that she did, because I don't think I would be sane if she hadn't. After all, little girls are not supposed to be treated like women.

By the time I was 15, I had been transferred between 25 homes. Yet, strangely enough, no one questioned why. Was it not because I had killed both my parents in their sleep and then methodically disposed of their bodies?

Not once did anyone question their 11-year-old daughter about the disappearance. Or why the carpet had dark red stains all over it. I often wondered why? Did they too know that my father had visited me every night and made me swear upon my life to never tell or I would die?

As I slide across a slippery spot on the hard-wood floor, a brief memory of last night flashes through my head before I fall on my ass in a puddle remarkably of still warm blood. "Damn it, I sure am making a fucking mess of this all." I think to myself before I push off the floor and head to the bathroom.

After fetching a few towels, I wipe up what I can of the blood before it gets in the creases of the wood planks, then I hurry to wrap up the body in the sheets. I do what I can before I hear a quick knock at the door. "Knock, knock." It comes again as I scan the room for some way to hide the evidence from the hallway.

"Knock, knock." Someone knocks several more times and louder as if they are in a hurry.

Knowing that if I open the door in my current state I will be hauled away by the cops, I stand perfectly still and hope that they just go away. However, a second later, the knocking continues. This time it is proceeded by a man's familiar deep voice stating urgently, "Open up. I know you are in there. I saw you go in with an older man."

While frantically scanning the room for a means of escape, I see the black curtains move as the breeze brushes them. Swallowing hard, I make a mad dash for the window before I hear a key in the lock and then the brass knob begins to turn slowly. I open the window the rest of the way and feel the wood under my fingers as I jump out before I even look to see what floor I am on.

Too late do I realize that I am on the second floor as I swallow hard and hope that I don't land too hard. Luckily, on my way down, a big lilac bush breaks my fall and I manage to escape with minimal cuts and bruises as I roll the rest of the way before landing on my feet, just as cats do.

As I hear someone yelling my name in the distance repeatedly, I run the opposite way and into the darkness. And when I find a big green dumpster just outside the back of the hotel, I climb inside quickly and close my eyes while I listen for anyone approaching. At first, I hear nothing, but as soon as someone finds the dead body, I begin to hear sirens surrounding the property in no time flat.

For the moment I stay put while I swallow hard and pray, because all I can do is hope that it dies down somewhat soon. After about a half hour of breathing through my mouth and sitting on the cold metal of the dumpster floor, I peek out a small crack in the lid. I see no movement, so I decide to make my move before someone finds me. After all, I need to get as far away from here as possible before the cop's corner off the area. Because once they do that, I will be trapped with no way out.

Unfortunately, while climbing out of the dumpster, I hear a noise behind me and then a flash of light as a cop car drives by slowly with its lights on bright. Wishing that I had waited just a few minutes longer, I shake my head, because I am about to get caught tonight. Of course, there is always a chance they won't see me.

"Yeah right." I murmur under my breath as I hunch down perfectly still and wait.

As soon as the cop car stops, I bolt for the refuge of the darkness and hope they don't trail after me. Of course, they always do, and this is when I hear that same deep familiar voice yelling hoarsely, "It wasn't her. I know that one. We have someone in custody already."

I feel the impulse to look, but the moment I turn to glance at him, all I see is his back. By the looks of it, he has let his hair grow out and hasn't been taking care of himself like he should have. But then again, I am not there to tell him differently. I also notice that his voice sounds dry as if he has been drinking again, and he seems to be struggling to keep upright. Not the same man I once knew. Of course, did I ever really know him?

Chapter 2: The Way I Like It

As I scan the room, I notice that a gentleman in the darkened corner by the bathrooms, has on a long, black overcoat. His blonde hair is short with spikes, and it contrasts with his dark-grey button-down shirt, of which can barely be seen. His dress pants are also black as well.

When I stare at him a little too long, I catch a glimpse of movement next to me. Then I feel the warmth of a hand slinking around my waist before it lowers to slide across my ass. No more than a second later, I hear a man's voice ask, "May I buy you a drink, gorgeous?"

Because I am taken by surprise, I turn around quickly and backhand him as I stare into a beautiful pair of baby blue eyes. This is usually my first response to someone who sneaks up behind me, so when it happens, I am not a bit surprised. However, he sure is. Especially, when my hand connects with his nose, and it emits a loud crunching noise as the bone breaks.

He cries out loudly, "You bitch!" as his hand quickly raises to his face and his other withdraws from my rear as he glares at me hatefully with blood dripping from his nose.

Not wanting more attention than I already created, I high tail it out of the bar and make my way to the car before I hear a man's voice calling out loudly, "Hey there. Just wait a minute."

I ignore him while I hurriedly unlock my red Toyota Camry before anyone else can come up behind me. However, a second later when I feel yet another man's hand on me, I turn around quickly to see that it is the gentleman from the corner. He is staring at me intensely with a glint in his eyes.

"Are you deaf or something?" The man asks with a baritone voice as he releases my shoulder and then fakes a smile.

While taking my eyes off him for a brief moment to scan the parking lot, I say seductively in almost a whisper, "No, I am not. However, if you want to come back to my place, I can show you what I am."

His eyes widen as he glances down at me with a smirk spreading on his lips, then a thought crosses my mind fleetingly, "I know this man from somewhere. But exactly where is the question?"

With a puzzled look on my face, I furrow my brow and offer my hand to him, only to have him reject me while stating snidely, "I would rather keep my head, than to get a moments pleasure before dying."

A nervous laugh escapes my lips as I turn my attention away from him and back to the car. This is clearly a mistake, because a second later, I feel the icy chill of a steel blade on me. It slides down the length of my lower arm as it scrapes the skin ever so gently. After realizing too late where I have seen him before, I swallow hard, then I quickly turn in the opposite direction. As I move effortlessly, I knock the blade out of his fist. I raise my right hand to jab him, before my knuckles collide with his cheek and completely throw him off guard for a good two seconds. However, as soon as he figures out what has happened, he hits me in return. As the blood sprays from my split lip, a Cheshire cat smile spreads across them and I whisper, "Is that all you got?"

I go to swing at him, but his fist closes around mine before I can move it. So, I spit a mix of blood and mucus into his face as I prepare for what comes next. When he slams me up against the car with his full weight, he holds me still as I bite down hard on his lip. And before he thrusts his tongue in between mine, I close my eyes because this is the way I have played this game so many times before. The next thing I know, we are inside the car and my panties are down as I feel his cock, balls deep inside of me.

I cry out, as my orgasm begins to build. My perfectly manicured nails sink deep into the sweaty skin of his neck as I tighten around his swollen shaft. And as I stare into his eyes, he keeps relentlessly pounding me with his hands wrapped tightly around my neck, squeezing, until I feel a surge of hot cum fill me completely. While he keeps pounding through it, I feel my own orgasm take control of my body. I close my eyes again as I watch the brilliant light display before it disappears. After watching him slide out, I swallow hard and then stare intently at his thick, rock-hard member as he strokes himself slowly for another round.

Little does he know that I have a skinning knife in my purse, just a mere inch away from my fingertips and I am ready to dispose of him at any time.

"I want to fuck you in every orifice. Matter of fact, by the time I get done with you, you won't be able to walk straight for at least a week. Not to mention, that no other man will ever feel half as good as I do." He says gruffly as he closes his eyes to stroke the tip before he moans.

That is precisely when I reach into my purse and strike. As I lash out, the cold metal slices right through his flesh like butter. I smile when it happens, because I love that feeling and that is precisely why I always keep my knives so sharp that they can cut through just about anything, including bone. As he gazes down at me helplessly, a look of shock spreads across his face before I see the realization of what has just happened. He tries to cry out and when he can't, he brings his cum covered hands to his throat. He tries again to say something, but all that comes out is a steady gurgling from his throat when the blood erupts from the wound. As I stare at him in amusement, bright red blood spews from his lips before I watch his life leave his eyes. "Now this is entertainment boys and girls." I think to myself excitedly before I begin to get annoyed.

While flicking the stray strand of brown hair out of my eyes, I wipe the blood off my lips and then push him over to the left side of the car so I can gather my things. As I figure out what to do next, I realize that I must drive the car somewhere so I can clean it up before anyone sees anything suspicious and reports it to the police. When I shake my head slowly, I pull down my black mini skirt and straighten my blouse before I scan the area cautiously. As I do, I look out the passenger side, back window, and notice that the coast is clear, so I open the door slowly. After all, the last thing I want is to bring attention to what just happened. Then I drive to an undisclosed location deep within the woods surrounding the metropolitan area, before dumping the body in the swamp and heading to the garage to clean up the car.

Once everything has been bagged and tagged, and I have changed my clothes, I hide my souvenir under the loose brick in the back wall of the garage. While making sure that I haven't forgotten anything before heading back to my apartment complex, I look over the car another time before I put it into gear and drive home. As soon as I pull in the parking lot, I see an all too familiar face and force myself to fake a smile before she strolls up to my door.

"Hey, Joanna. You look like you just got fucked!" Tina Sampson exclaims with a little bit of a slur to her voice.

I can already tell that she has been drinking tonight and alcohol does not make her any more attractive than she was before. Instead, her 38-year-old steel grey eyes are droopy now and her long, straight blonde hair has become tangled. As I glance over her clothes, I notice that her white T-shirt has a dark red wine stain on it at the collar.

"And you look like you have had entirely too much to drink." I reply sarcastically as I roll my eyes at her in hopes of making her go away.

Unfortunately, it achieves the exact opposite effect, as she stands there staring at me with her hands on her hips. While beginning to pout, she murmurs under her breath, "Must she always be such a bitch?"

Clearing my throat, I open the door and grab my purse before I state flatly, "Yes." within an inch of her face.

As I stand there, staring her down, I fight the urge to reach into my purse and slit her throat right where she stands, but I don't because that would make things even more complicated. Upon hearing the two new neighbors fighting over what color of couch to get behind me, I can't help but to laugh at something so trivial, when less than an hour earlier I cleaned up a murder scene. If they only knew that their neighbor was the killer in the papers, they surely would shit themselves and run as far away as possible. Instead, they are completely oblivious of everything going on around them and that is exactly the way I want to keep it. Especially, when Miss Goody Two Shoes doesn't have the guts to do what is needed to keep her safe.

Chapter 3: Lucy

After slamming the door in Tina's face, I come out of hiding and Joanna disappears for the moment as I peel off my clothes and decide to take a luxurious bath with my play toy. On the way, I clean up the discarded items of clothing off the hardwood floor and notice something strange by the door. I don't know how I didn't see it when I walked in, unless I was so preoccupied with the fact that Joanna had just killed again, that I just completely missed it. After I cock my head, I stand up and walk over to the piece of white folded up notebook paper that looks like someone just jotted a quick note on it, before sliding it underneath my door.

"How odd." I murmur under my breath as I turn it over and then see my real name on it in fancy handwriting.

"Who on earth knows my real name still?" I think to myself as I unfold the paper and then I smell the sweet fragrance of my mother's perfume. Lilacs. I remember it so well as if it was just yesterday. She always wore it when they went out on their dates. It was her favorite scent in the whole wide world.

While recalling one specific time when I was 9, I begin to shrink a little when I remember what always came afterwards. Always. As a matter of fact, when I began to bleed, it didn't stop him. Instead, it seemed to fuel him on like a monster in a nightmare. After remembering that sick smile on his face when Joanna left, I slam my fist into the wall by my head violently with tears in my eyes.

I will always remember how men treat me, but then again, I have Joanna, and she always takes good care of me. For the longest time she was my hero, and I think that is why I decided to take on her name when I ran away. It was a decision I was forced to make when my last foster family, the Smith's, decided I was too hard to handle. They were going to throw me back into the system where I had been for many years, and I could not let that happen.

As I look over the handwritten note, I begin to worry. However, the moment I read the last sentence, I realize that I am fucked. Someone knows who I really am and that is not a good thing. Now, how do I find them and get them to disappear?

After turning the folded note over in my hands, I notice a small mark at the bottom and raise it closer to my eyes. I squint my eyes to focus on it before I realize that it is a triangle logo for a company on the upper east side. Once I note that I can get there in 20 minutes flat, I begin to formulate a plan. After all, it is far too late tonight. But in the morning, I can be there when it first opens so no one else will see me there. That is, of course, in case Joanna needs to dispose of yet another body later.

While rolling my eyes, I fold the note back up and sigh before placing it gently on the blue card table that I use as a replacement for my kitchen table. Then I head towards the bathroom once again while rubbing the back of my neck softly with my right hand. I begin to wrack my brain for a memory, or a face, but nothing comes to mind. Instead, where a memory should be, there is nothing.

"Is this someone that Joanna has met?" I suddenly think to myself before stepping into the bathroom.

When I walk up to the white pedestal sink, I find myself wondering if this is someone from my past who knows what Joanna has done. Or are they merely trying to see if I will run? Either way, after I find out what this company knows, I will need to think about what to do next calmly and while staying completely in control.

As I turn on the icy water, I brush my teeth and stare into the mirror at my reflection. I had forgotten how long my hair had become, because when Joanna takes over, time tends to stand still for me. Sometimes I even lose my memories. I guess in a way, it feels like I drift off to sleep, then I watch as if I'm in a dream when she takes over and does her thing.

After I brush my teeth to the count of 100 obsessively, I spit out the toothpaste and then pick up my water glass before rinsing out my mouth. A moment later, I glance back into the mirror and stare into my green eyes. I could swear I see Joanna staring back at me for a split second and this unnerves me because she is always there, even when I don't need her. However, when I feel my muscles twinge, I remember why I came into the bathroom in the first place.

I swallow hard as I walk over to the bathtub and lean down before turning the hot water on. Right away, the steam starts to rise from the tub as it fills it so slowly. In anticipation, I smile wickedly and then

I sit down on the edge of the tub to dip one toe in carefully. The water is piping hot, so I wince while quickly withdrawing my foot, then I turn the cold faucet on to cool it down a little.

The moment I hear something just outside the window, I stand up. Then I walk over to the baby blue see-through curtain before I pull it to the side and watch as a tree branch taps on the windowpane. "Tap, tap." it continues to tap on the window until it stops suddenly for absolutely no reason.

At the same time, I look out into the darkness as I feel strange for some reason. It is as if someone unseen is staring right back at me and if I look close enough, it may show itself. The mere thought of it chills me to the bone as I step back quickly and turn to see the water starting to overflow from the bathtub.

"Shit!" I exclaim while hurrying to shut the water off, then I reach down into the tub to pull the plug and drain some of the water.

When I stand back up, I hear another strange noise at the window, but decide that I would rather be in the water than to let my fears take control. So, I slip in carefully and slide down the back of the tub. I immerse myself completely from head to toe in the most wonderful feeling in the world. And as the hot water envelopes me, I still feel like there is someone watching me from the window. However, strangely enough I don't care as I reach over for my Pleasure 3000 with a sly smirk on my lips.

The moment I feel the vibration on my clit, I close my eyes and begin to moan because it feels so good that I could easily cum in a matter of minutes. I sigh as I slowly insert it in between my engorged folds. The skin there is so sensitive that I feel every little movement, every inch of cool plastic as it fills me.

When I run my left hand up over my silky skin to my pebbled left nipple, I pinch it and then cry out in ecstasy. Then I begin to play with my toy in and out steadily. As I thrust it in, I turn it from side to side and then pull it out at an increasing pace. For a few minutes longer, I keep thrusting in and out while I lick my lips and pinch my nipple between my thumb and forefinger tightly until I can no longer handle it.

I cry out in need while I thrust it in once more as I release my nipple and then move my fingers to my nub. I pinch it hard and thrust in again and again until I feel my orgasm take hold. As I watch the brilliant light display from under my eyelids, I moan in satisfaction while shaking and thrusting through it. Afterwards, I sigh deeply because now the water is beginning to get cold, so I withdraw my play toy and climb out of the tub.

After wrapping the soft, white towel around my body tightly, I shut off the light to the bathroom and head to bed.

Chapter 4: Jon Harrison

While standing outside Joanna Michaels' bathroom window in the darkness, I begin to feel like I shouldn't be here, even though it is literally part of my job. As a matter of fact, the captain just put me on this case tonight and I already feel as if I am intruding into something special. So, when I see her standing naked in her bathroom window, I quickly stop the branch from hitting the window so she will turn away. I sigh before swallowing hard when the curtain falls, and she turns around as I catch one more glimpse of the most beautiful woman I have ever seen.

After she is in the bathroom for about 30 minutes give or take, I watch as she shuts off all the lights methodically. Now mind you, I wouldn't have minded seeing what she was up to for so long in there, but I kept it professional and stayed within limits. When I look down at my watch and then back up at her window, I notice that all is quiet in her small apartment on the upper west side of the city. Eventually, I walk back to the car and wait for morning so I can report back to the captain on the relatively little that I could. After all, the whole time I was watching her, I only saw one suspicious thing and it wasn't even of her doing.

Earlier that night, just a few minutes after I watched her enter the apartment, I noticed something very strange indeed. An older woman in her 50's with greying, brown hair, and a limp, walked into the apartment complex. No more than a minute later, she briskly rushed back out again after scanning the parking lot. When I went to grab my phone to take a picture, I looked down and then back up before noticing that she had disappeared into thin air like a ghost.

Puzzled by this, I began to wonder if she had anything to do with Joanna. If she did, who exactly was she? Is she another serial killer? Or could she be her mother?

Upon hearing a loud noise coming from a few feet away, I quickly open my eyes and realize that I have been asleep. "Shit! Captain Donahue will have my balls if he finds out that I was asleep on the job again." I murmur under my breath as I narrow my eyes to see through the glare from the sunrise.

When I hear the noise again, I spot what is causing it immediately this time as it hits my window and almost crashes right through it. A second later, the crow hits the ground as I stare at it flopping around with a broken wing and blood speckled all over its feathers. As it looks up at me, I feel a twinge of sympathy but then decide better because what if she were to come out right now and see me sitting here. I could never live it down if they had to transfer me off this case too.

After all, being a washed-up homicide detective at the age of 32 is never a good thing. Especially, when I don't have a clue what I would do as a regular citizen in the private sector. Although, I suppose I could always fall back on my father's money or the fact that I have a college degree in business. But what fun would any of that be, honestly?

So, as I sit here contemplating if I should put this bird out of its misery or if I need to stay put, I realize that Ms. Joanna Michaels is awake and staring at me through her open kitchen window. After glancing away from her quickly, I pretend that I am waiting for someone, so she doesn't figure out that I am really spying on her and getting so close to figuring out where she hides the bodies.

I could swear that last night as I sat in this very parking lot, she was out on a date with death. Because when she came back, she looked like someone who had something to hide. As for myself, I would be lying if I said I didn't have a few skeletons in my closet, but mine are dead and buried, far from prying eyes. I don't think I have ever told anyone my secrets, and I would prefer keeping it that way if I could.

When I look back at her stealthily, I notice that she is out of sight and for the first time in my life, I feel a sense of ease as I sit here in silence. Normally, I can't stop myself from needing to move, and do something. However, in this instance, a sense of calm over comes me as I close my eyes and see the image of her naked body in my mind.

This is a woman who I wouldn't mind filling completely and then sleeping next to with one eye open always. Of course, that will never happen because the Department has very strict policies about fraternizing with the suspects. Even if they didn't, I don't think I would be caught in that position because the results could be literally deadly.

As I look down at my watch a few minutes later, I realize that I am off duty and the next detective in charge should be here at any moment. However, when 9 a.m. rolls around and he still hasn't shown up, I begin to wonder and call it in.

"Captain, Detective Reynolds didn't show up this morning. What do you want me to do?" I ask hesitantly because I really don't need to be on his shit list.

"Well, first of all, is the woman still at her apartment?" He asks as if he really has something else on his mind and he could care less.

"Yes, she is." I say quietly to make sure no one hears me as I scan the area and then glance up at her tiny apartment window.

This is certainly not the best part of town, but at least it isn't in the projects.

"Alright, then come back to the precinct and fill out your paperwork. I want to know everything that has happened since you arrived. There has got to be a way we can pin her for this. Do you understand?" He says angrily before hanging up.

After I look down and see that he has ended the call, I glance up at her window one more time and notice that the lights are shut off. Then, I see her rush out to her car with her long brown hair tied up in a ponytail, before putting her car in reverse and backing up, almost into mine. As she leaves in a hurry, I spot her staring into her rearview mirror and puckering her bright red lips at me seductively.

When I realize that now is my chance, I take off after her but manage to keep a safe distance, so she doesn't realize that I am tailing her.

Chapter 5: Aunt Anita

When I end up in the upper east side of the city, I slowly drive through each street, until I arrive at my destination and pull up in front of the Ice INC. building on 25th street. Several times on the way, I catch myself searching behind me in the rearview mirror because I keep feeling like someone is following me. Of course, the only thing I see is a black sedan that may or may not be the same one that was in my parking lot earlier.

Now, I suppose he could be tailing me. If so, Joanna may have to do something about him later if he poses a threat. We will just wait and see, but for the moment I need to take care of something else that is more pressing. While pulling the note out of my little black purse, I straighten out my pink mini-skirt and open my car door before a man who looks to be no older than 23 with freckles and red hair, walks up and looks expectantly at me with his hand held out.

As I look down, it finally dawns on me what he wants, so I give him my keys and then reach back into my purse for a crisp $50 bill before handing it to him. His eyes glance down and then he nods at me approvingly while I watch him move towards my girl. Now, I usually never trust anyone with my old car, but this time it is unavoidable as I watch him drive her away. While reaching for the door, I hear a woman behind me ask softly, "Lucy? Lucy Johnson?"

When I turn around slowly, I come face to face with my aunt Anita of all people. After I killed my parents, she had always suspected that I did it, so she did not want to take me in. Instead, she turned me over to the foster care system, where I had it worse than most girls my age because I was prettier and had bigger breasts.

It was truly a shame, because I think if she had a hand in raising me, I really don't think I would have turned out the way that I did. Or at least I hope I wouldn't have.

"Yes." I say in almost a whisper as I narrow my eyes and furrow my brow.

Stepping back, I look both ways in case I need to bolt. However, she takes my hand and leads me away from the building and into the dark alley next to it. As I stare at her cautiously, I wonder if she is the one who left me the note and why.

When we come to a stop, she turns around and stares at me for a long time before ever saying a word. It is uncomfortable, but at the same time, I am glad because I wouldn't have a clue what to say in the first place.

"Lucy, I am so sorry about all those years ago. I know I should have done something, but at that time, I was so grief stricken that I couldn't come to terms with their disappearance. It was as if they had never really existed in the first place." She says with tears in her eyes as she stares at the ground.

Swallowing hard, I notice that she is still holding my hand before I raise my voice and reply, "It was a long time ago. No need to rehash it. I have grown and moved on from what had happened. I guess in a way you could say it made me the person I am today."

As she releases me slowly, she steps back and looks me up and down before saying softly, "My, you have grown into a lovely young lady. If my eyes don't deceive me, I could swear you look just like your mother did at your age. You could almost be her twin."

Not realizing that, I fake a smile and silently think about this for a moment in reflection before commenting sweetly, "You don't look too bad yourself for a woman of your age."

Ignoring my comment, she glances out at the street behind me before saying in a hushed voice, "I needed to see you one last time. I am dying and I don't have long to live. It was hard to track you down, but I understand why you changed your name. It is often hard to outrun your past and I know what you did."

As I raise my left eyebrow, I swallow hard before threatening in a whisper, "I did what I did out of a will to survive. Nothing more or nothing less. I suggest you leave and never come back, or the same fate may be yours as well."

The moment she hears this, a sick smile spreads across her lips and then she says, "I always knew you did it. I just had no proof until now."

When she produces a tape recorder from her pocket, I look down at the small grey instrument in her hands and immediately knock it to the ground. The pieces shatter everywhere, and the tape is thrown into the brush by the wall. I glance back at her threateningly before stating in a growl, "How dare you! Do you not know what my father did all those years to me as a small child? Do you condone this? If so, you are no better than they were and deserve to die as much as they did."

Moving towards her quickly, I slam her against the wall and then glare into her eyes from a mere two inches away. I poke my finger into her chest and say hatefully, "Bitch, if I ever see you again, I will tear you from limb to limb. I don't care if you are my aunt. You have never acted like one to me. Now get."

As soon as she hears these words, her eyes widen as she realizes that I mean what I say. While she struggles to get free, she pushes against me before I let her up and away from me. After I watch her rush out of the alley, I quickly walk over to the place that the tape fell and retrieve it before placing it in my purse for safe keeping.

Chapter 6: Officially Meeting Jon Harrison

Upon returning to the front of the building, I have the young man fetch my car and then I decide on the way home to stop at the grocery store for my next few meals. As I walk through the store, I notice a familiar face and realize that he must be stalking me, or he is with the police force. Either way, I need to be more careful in everything I do. I should not have done what I did regarding my aunt. That may come back to haunt me one day, I just know it.

Once I pay for my food, I glance behind me to see the man still trailing from a far, even though he is making it less than obvious now. Seeing that he isn't paying attention to me as he pulls out his money from his back pocket, I make a break for it and rush to my car. However, before I can pull out of the parking lot, he is already in his vehicle and right behind me, blocking me from leaving.

I watch him step out of the car and as soon as he is within a few feet of me, my senses go in overdrive as I get a good look at him and lick my chops. He looks tasty at 6 foot and boy is he built. His muscles pop out of his partially unbuttoned red-plaid flannel shirt as they flex, then I look up and become enchanted by his eyes. They are an alarmingly beautiful color of greenish-blue and now they are trained on me like a hawk watching its prey.

While knocking on my window, he smiles charmingly before I open it and I ask innocently, "Can you please move your vehicle? It is right in my way."

His smile turns to a grin as he looks down my shirt at my cleavage and then his eyes return to mine before replying curiously enough, "Actually, I had seen you in the store. To be honest, I stopped you to ask you out tonight. I know it is stupid of me, but you don't have a boyfriend or a husband by chance, do you?"

Shaking my head unconsciously, I realize that Joanna is taking over and sure enough I watch from the sidelines as she seductively answers, "No, want to try out for the position?"

As soon as she says it, he grins smugly and then replies in almost a whisper, "Sure baby. Where do you live?"

"I live on the upper west side, but right now my landlord is in the middle of doing renovations. Why don't we go to a motel I know just down the road from here? They rent by the hour." I say casually as I scan the area around us.

"Hm. By the hour? I thought that we could take it nice and slow. I might need a whole day and night for what I have planned." He says while licking his lips slowly and then handing me his phone.

"Why don't you put your name and phone number in my contacts so I can call you later this afternoon. I might have a place where we can spend some quality time getting to know each other better." He adds as I begin to type Christy in his phone and then the number to my disposable that I purchased for this exact situation if it ever was needed.

Although, I stop when I realize that he is avoiding his house for some reason and that makes me annoyed. Turning to him before I hand him his phone, I ask innocently, "But why not your place? You don't have a wife or a girlfriend, do you? I don't like two timers. They turn me completely off."

"No, no. Of course not!" He exclaims playfully as he takes a step back before answering quickly, "I just don't like taking women back to my place when I don't know them. I have had women stalk me before and they have even gone so far to make sure that no other woman gets near me."

"Really?" I ask because now I am curious and want to hear his sordid tales about his crazy ex-lovers.

Now leaning closer, I begin to tap my perfectly manicured nails on the window, as I say softly, "You know. I am beginning to think that we are two of a kind."

"Hm. I certainly hope so, because I was just thinking that I wouldn't mind parking somewhere right now and finding out just how snugly I fit inside that sweet little pussy of yours." He replies in a deep voice before licking his lips and staring hungrily at my hard nipples.

"I don't know if either one of our cars has room enough for me to ride you like the bucking bronco that you are." I say before smiling seductively and then I bite my lip as I think about slitting his throat after we have sex.

There is just nothing like feeling warm blood flowing over your fingers as you watch their last breath leave their lips. When they cease to exist, their eyes turn glossy and grey as the light leaves from within them. What I like the most though, is when I slice off their earlobe and then roll it between my fingertips. After I produce a sandwich bag from my purse, I always put the earlobe into it before I insert the baggy into the special compartment in the bottom of my purse for safe keeping.

"You have no idea. I want to fuck you six ways from Sunday and if given the chance, I will make sure you never forget me.' He says before a smirk plays on his lips.

"Well, then let me know when you are ready and I will take you up on it, happily sugar." I promise as I flutter my eyelashes at him and then watch him take a few steps back.

He looks down at his phone and then states quickly, "I must go for now, but that is a date. As a matter of fact, I will call you with the details in a couple of hours. Alright?"

While nodding, I fake a smile and then lick my lower lip slowly before running my finger over the neckline of my shirt. I watch as his eyes follow my every move, only to stop at my breasts and stare wan tingly for a moment before stating breathlessly, "Well, I must go. Talk to you in a few."

The whole time he is walking back to his car, I watch him like a hawk, because honestly, I don't trust him one bit. There is something about him that screams "bad news" and if I am not careful, I might end up getting caught this time.

Chapter 7: Been There And Done That

After the man with no name walks back to his car, I realize that he had never given it to me in the first place. Which is just as well, because I didn't intend on ever going through with whatever he had in mind anyways. However, as soon as he opens his driver side door suddenly, he stops in place and then I watch as he shakes his head. Turning around, he walks back to me casually before knocking on my rolled-up window expectantly.

When I grab the chrome handle to open it just an inch or two, I glance up into those damn gorgeous eyes of his and then lose my train of thought for a moment while I silently hate myself for feeling weak. I hesitate and then roll it down before I smile at him seductively. Honestly, I don't think I have ever felt this way about a single man in my life. It is quite strange, because I just met him, and I don't have a clue what is going on. It both irritates me beyond belief but piques my curiosity as well.

"Excuse me, I just realized that I never told you, my name. I'm Jon Harrison. Your name is Christy, right? That is a pretty name. Anyway, I need to get going. I will call you in a bit when I know more." He says softly as he apologizes and then grins.

Nodding, I don't really know what to say, so I leave it at that. And as I watch him rush back to his car, I turn the key before I hear the engine roar to life. After I hit the button on the radio, I listen to a soulful deep voice as the vocalist sings about heart break and lost love. It should have struck a chord, but I still only feel the coldness of my nonexistent heart.

On the way home, she leaves me finally while I begin to wonder who exactly this man is. He has already had such a strong effect on me. Is he the detective who will put me behind bars? Or is he someone I can trust with my secrets once and for all without having to kill him? If so, what will he think of my past time and will he think I will do the same to him as well? So many questions and no real answers to fill the void as I sit in the car and contemplate what my next move shall be with this man if he calls.

As soon as I return home, I scan the parking lot slowly and do not see the black sedan. I let out a big sigh, before I see that there is a dark tan moving van just outside the apartment complex that has on it in big, blocky red letters, Billy's Painting Service on the back. A dopey looking man holds a paintbrush on the side of it, and as I stare, I struggle not to laugh.

"Hm. I wonder." I murmur under my breath as I run my forefinger over my lower lip slowly and think.

While wondering if this could be the detectives, I quickly climb out of the car and walk up to the building quite normally. I check the mail and then I glance over at the van before heading inside. As soon as I unlock the door to my apartment, I hear a noise behind me and then turn to see Nick walking up quickly. "Hey gorgeous." He whispers in my ear before running his fingers over my shoulders tenderly.

"What's up?" I ask softly as I glare at his hazel eyes and wonder what he could possibly be up to.

"How about some lunch and then a quick fuck?" He suggests as his eyes lower to my breasts slowly.

"Nick. You know as well as I do, that this will never happen." I say while sighing and then giving the door a gentle shove after turning the brass nob in my hand.

After running his fingers through his long blonde bangs, he says sadly, "Yeah, well I thought I would try. You must give me credit for that. Right? One of these days."

When his voice trails off, he looks to the end of the hall where Ms. Davison is carrying three large bags of groceries. My eyes follow his as I notice her.

"It must be grocery day for both of us." I think to myself as I pick up my two bags and then walk inside.

Suddenly, I turn around and say to Nick hesitantly, "Perhaps, some time I will take you up on that." Before I shut the door gently and put the bags down on the floor in front of me.

While leaning against the back of the door, I close my eyes because this is exhausting, and I don't know how much more of this I can handle.

"Nick needs to get the point. He is a good kid, but I am not into surfers. He really needs to grow up and get over himself." I murmur to myself before adding slowly, "Of course. I don't think I would mind his face between my legs, just once. But I can't chance her coming out to play."

As I shake my head, I open my eyes with a sly smirk on my lips, before I pick up the grocery bags and walk into the cozy little kitchen with blue cloud print wallpaper.

"It is one of my few happy places." I think to myself before I place the bags on the marble countertop.

Afterwards, I begin to sift through the various items and then put them away where they belong. One thing I do not notice until I have put everything in its place is the fact that I left my purse in the car as well. And when I realize it, I sigh because I don't really want to walk all the way back there. However, when I remember that my phone is also out there, I begin to swear under my breath deliberately, "motherfucker."

Now, I must go to the car to get them because that man may call, and I don't want to miss it. Honestly, I don't know if it is because I am attracted to him, or the fact that I need to know if he is trailing me. Either way, I force myself to go out and get them. The moment I step out the doors, and look around the parking lot, I notice that the moving van is gone and now the black sedan is back.

While taking a chance, I walk closer to the car than I should and look in to see that there is an older gentleman sitting there with a wide brimmed white hat on. He is talking loudly on the phone as if he is aggravated by the person on the other side of the conversation. As he quickly glancing at me, he frowns and furrows his brow before putting his car into reverse and backing up as he leaves.

Good thing, because if he was the same man from earlier, I might have to get in the car with him and then she would make him conveniently disappear. I roll my eyes as I watch him leave and then walk back into the complex, while skirting around Nick's place. After all, the last thing I need right now is him on my tail again. I think I have had enough flirting for a lifetime at this rate.

After returning to the refuge of my apartment, I sigh and shrug my shoulders before I make myself a bologna sandwich. Then I walk to the table and sit down to do a little research while taking my first bite hungrily. As I open my laptop slowly, I type the license plate number into the police database and wait a few minutes for the process to complete. When I hear it ding, I look down and then see it.

"Surprise, surprise. It is not legal." I say out loud to an empty room as I furrow my brow and wonder who it is then.

"Of course." I say as I smack myself in the forehead a moment later with the palm of my hand.

How could I be so stupid? The department is surely not going to put a real plate on their surveillance cars. That would be far too easy to trace, like I just did. After closing the lid of the computer,

I eat the rest of the sandwich and stand up before stretching my arms up towards the ceiling. Then I grab my plate and take it to the sink before leisurely walking into the living room.

As I watch Tomorrow Will Never Be, I open the ice-cold bottle of water and swallow a mouthful. Then I realize that for once, I am content for the moment. "How odd? I can't remember the last time that I have been able to really relax, let alone sit back and finish the rest of the movie with my feet up on the coffee table." I think to myself as I raise my left eyebrow.

A moment later, I begin to yawn before picking up my favorite book and settling in for a couple of hours.

Chapter 8: The Phone Call

I must have fallen asleep sometime in the afternoon while reading. Because when I hear the phone ring, it startles me, so I sit up while feeling dazed. I look around slowly and realize that I won't reach it before it goes to voice mail.

"Damn it!" I exclaim as the phone falls to the hard-wood floor.

"Why on earth did it have to do that? Now I must figure out who called." I think to myself as I rub my shoulder tenderly and work out the soreness in my muscles.

As I reach down to grab my phone, it begins to ring again. Once again it startles me, but this time I manage to answer it before I hear my voice say sarcastically, "I am not home right now…"

After I take a deep breath, I answer it by stating quickly, "I am here." Before I ever scan the phone to see who has called.

When I do look down at the screen, I notice that there is only a number and no name. How odd?

"I told you I would give you a call. So, I may have found a place. How about we meet up in an hour for dinner and then what we do afterwards is totally up to you." He says hesitantly while sounding like he is doing something else in the background.

"Alright. Where do we meet and when exactly? I would hate to be late for our first date." I say sweetly like a schoolgirl, before clearing my throat and asking slyly, "If that is what this is?"

"But of course. I wouldn't have it any other way. However, if you want to forego dinner and go straight to the evening's activities, I will be all in for that too. But, be warned, I am just a little hungry. So, my stomach may or may not start to growl while I am in the middle of eating you out." He says sarcastically before his voice trails off.

While wondering if he meant what he said, I decide that we probably should go out to eat first just to be safe. Besides, the fact that my stomach is already growling means that if I don't eat first, I won't even make it to first base before wishing that I had.

"Let's meet up at the corner of 5th and Brooks Street at 6 p.m. The restaurant parking lot is usually full, and that is just down the street from it. Is that alright?" He asks thoughtfully before he waits patiently for my reply with a breathlessness to his voice.

"Yes, yes of course it is. A little walk never hurts anyone. After all, it will just make us hungrier." I say before a smile seductively and stand up to stretch.

"That sounds good to me. Anyways, I need to get a few things done before we meet. See you then?" He asks hesitantly before all I hear is silence on the phone.

"Yes, it is a date. See you soon." I reply softly while thinking about what to wear.

After making sure that the call has ended, I glance down at my screen and then put it in my pocket. As I walk to the bedroom, I can't help but wonder if he is the real thing. Or if he is playing with me like Joanna often plays with her toys?

While shaking my head, I decide it is best to not think about this too hard as I walk in the door to the bedroom and scan the room for something, but I don't know what. When I see it, I smile and then rush over to the dresser where a pair of blue heart shape, Diamond earrings, lay on the top. The silver posts glitter in the light as the sunset filters in through the window.

My favorite time of day, right before dark when the sunset looks the prettiest. Just before the sun disappears behind the tree line and then the dark descends upon the world. It is right at this moment that I remember something my mother used to say when I was a small child. "Come here Lucy dear. Now, remember when a man asks you to marry him, what do we say?"

I would always reply like a good little daughter as I mimicked her, "What do I get out of this?" then she would add with a seriousness to her voice, "Never forget that. If there is one thing men want, it is a woman who doesn't give them lip. If you do and he still wants you, then he is a keeper."

Sometimes, I often wondered if my mother hated me because my father wanted me and not her. Could that have been why she always said this? Who knows?

While walking towards my closet, I pass the full-length mirror on the wall and notice that I seem to be getting skinner by the minute. I knew that I hadn't been eating like I should, but living like this must be taking more of a toll on me than I knew.

As I walk into the closet area, I begin to go through each of my outfits until I find a pretty little red dress and matching panties. They are silky and feel so nice against my skin when I put them on one by one. Before I step into my dress, I sit down on the edge of the bed and roll up my first black stocking, then the other. These are my favorite kind because they have an elastic top that holds them in place, so no need for a belt and they look so much nicer.

Once I have them both on, I run my fingers over the silky softness before I pick up the dress in both hands. I lower it down so I can step into it easily enough and then I pull it up and over my chest.

"Just right." I murmur under my breath as I admire my reflection in the mirror.

Now comes the best part. I put in the earrings.

"Absolutely beautiful." I say as I admit it to myself.

After I admire myself one more time while turning around, I glance up at the round white clock on my wall and then exclaim, "Shit! I need to go, or I will be late."

While grabbing my purse quickly, I hightail it for the parking lot by the restaurant and hope that a cop doesn't decide to stop me along the way.

Chapter 9: Something Is Different

Just before I drive into the parking lot, I notice the line for the restaurant is almost around the block. I begin to wonder and think to myself, "I sure hope that he does have a reservation, because otherwise we will be at the end of it, and I won't be happy at all." Neither will my stomach because it is currently growling loudly at the mere thought of food.

After driving around two times, I finally find a spot towards the rear and park while I still can. As I get out of the car, I hear a familiar voice from behind me say warmly, "Christy, I had my doubts that you were going to come, but I am sure glad you did."

I turn around and smile as Jon walks up to me as casually as can be while my heart leaps up into my throat nervously.

"I was weighing my options, but then my stomach had the ultimate say so the minute it wouldn't stop growling." I say jokingly as I flutter my eyelashes at him and make sure that he can see plenty of cleavage while I bend forward a little.

"Mhm. I really do appreciate it." He says softly as he practically drools all over himself.

I can't help but laugh as I watch him stare at my breasts so hungrily.

"You know. If I wasn't so damn hungry, I would forego it and suck on this instead." I state seductively as I step closer to him before running my fingers down to the rather significant bulge in his pants.

When I feel his cock twitch and pulsate in my hand, I smirk and then lick my lower lip as I dare to stare him in the eyes. At this moment, I want to fuck him more than I want the steak I have been dying to try. And even though my stomach keeps growling, I run my hand back up, then I push him against the car as I stand threateningly close to him.

I keep eye contact with him as I lean in on my tip toes before I kiss him firmly on the lips. At first, he does nothing, so I flirt with him by biting his lip before going in for the kill. As it just so happens, it tastes like honey with a hint of spice. The whole time we kiss, I can't seem to get the thought out of my mind that it strongly reminds me of rum or a brandy I had tried once as a teenager.

The moment I feel his arms surrounding me, I begin to get lightheaded, so I shove him backwards and stop. I shake my head and glance up at his face to see what is running through his mind right now. I just know that if I keep this up, I won't be in control for very much longer.

"Stop!" I cry out as I hold my hands in front of me.

Staring at me blankly, he blinks and then gazes into my eyes in confusion, before asking thoughtfully, "Didn't you want it to?"

Swallowing hard, I nod, and then answer softly, "Yes, but it is complicated. I am both hungry and confused, so can we please at least take care of the one for now? If I don't get any food, I am afraid I will expire."

I laugh and then there suddenly is an awkward silence between us as we start to walk towards the restaurant. On the way, he glances over at me several times as we walk next to each other casually, but he never says anything. I refuse to acknowledge the fact that he keeps looking at me like I am his dinner, because that can only mean that he will be dead within a few hours, and I rather like him.

There must be some way that I can stop her from taking over when I have sex. For once in my life, I want to feel what she does. I know before this it was purely a defense mechanism, but with this man I feel something different. It is almost as if we are two peas in a pod. It's really hard to explain for someone who has always been afraid of men and has lived her life running away every time she turns around.

The next time he looks at me, I finally admit that I know and then say sweetly, "You know, I don't bite. You can talk to me."

Afterwards there is another awkward silence for a minute or two as if he is trying to figure out what to say. Finally, he clears his throat and asks hesitantly, "You aren't a vegetarian, are you?"

I laugh again whole heartedly and then smile as I wink at him while replying seductively as I stare down at the bulge in his pants and then back up again to his gorgeous eyes, "No, I rather like my meat."

While laughing, he almost chokes and then he murmurs under his breath quietly, "Hm, seems that I have a comedian here."

Lashing out quickly, I smack him in the shoulder jokingly and then say sarcastically, "Oh come on. You know you want my lips wrapped around him. You know you want it."

Surprisingly, he stops in his tracks and turns to me before looking dead serious and stating flatly, "If you keep that up, I am going to take you in the bathroom and fill that smart mouth of yours with him, then we will see if you really mean what you say."

Smirking, I wink at him and then reply, "I did but I may bite him mistakenly because I am so hungry. Now, can we please continue to the restaurant?"

Looking ahead, I see the long line and then glance back at him before he says softly, "No worries."

As he takes my hand, we walk past the long line and make our way to the front. He smiles and then pats the attendant on the back before he takes him aside and speaks with him for a moment. When they return, he grins and then says sarcastically, "Ready sweetie?"

I laugh because I have no idea what he just said to the attendant, but it must have been a lie by the mischievous glint in his eyes. And when the door opens, we step inside before I become completely surprised. It is not at all like I expected. Instead, it is very modern and trendy and as I stare at the food on the tables, he leads the way while holding my hand until we reach our table.

When he holds the decorative steel chair out for me, I smile and then say in almost a whisper, "Thank you." before I take a seat and then watch him do the same.

The tables are different from what I am used to with see-through glass tops and steel legs that match the chairs. There is a crystal vase in the middle of the table with one solitary red long stemmed rose in it. Beautiful, I might add.

Smiling sweetly, I sit silently as I watch the attendant place a crisp white napkin in front of me and then all the shiny silverware in order. As she hurries to place his down, I glance over at her and notice that her long straight red hair is rather beautiful as it cascades over her shoulders. Her freckles are endearing, but her eyes are an emerald green which I have never seen before.

When she turns to look at me, I smile again and then ask curiously, "What is the special tonight?"

"I am glad you asked. The chef has prepared a lobster bisque with a biscuit on the side. Perhaps you may want some alfredo noodles too?" She asks as she watches me like a hawk.

"Yes, that sounds rather nice. Don't you think so?" I ask Jon sweetly as I turn to stare at him.

"Of course. It sounds wonderful. Can we also have two glasses of your best red house wine, please?" He asks pleasantly before smiling and laying his napkin over his lap.

Once everything has been ordered, the attendant walks away and then I find myself with a man staring at me intently in silence. I don't know what to say, so I stare back at him until he finally suggests in a whisper as he leans closer, "Let's go to the bathroom. I will go first and then you can meet me in the lady's room."

Chapter 10: The Rendezvous

That was exactly what I had been hoping he would suggest. Remarkably enough, when he says it in a whisper, I can't help but to feel like a young schoolgirl doing something forbidden. It sends a delicious shiver up my spine and instantly makes me wet. Somehow this man affects me like no other ever has. Perhaps, she won't feel the need to come out to protect me if I am truly enjoying myself for once.

He whispers quietly with a mischievous glint in his eyes, "See you in a few." Then he stands up quickly before walking casually to the bathrooms. I swallow hard as I look around me to make sure that no one is watching. Of course, no one is because they are all in their own little world, so I too stand up and then follow after him.

The moment I see a woman walking out of the lady's room with a disapproving look on her face, I already know that he is waiting for me inside. As I push the cold metal door open slowly, I see what I was looking for. He is standing next to the chrome sink with a Cheshire smile on his handsome face. The flickering fluorescent light is washing all the color out of his face, but he is still more handsome than any other man in the restaurant.

"Well, don't just stand there, shut the door behind you and follow me!" he exclaims a little louder now that we are alone for the time being.

A smirk plays slowly across my lips when I realize that he wants to fuck me as much as I want him to, so I quickly follow him inside. I manage to wedge myself next to him while he locks the door to the stall. Even though it is cramped, it is more than big enough for our intents and purposes.

"Mm, baby, if I didn't know better, I would think that you are already wet and willing." he whispers right next to my ear as I feel his hot breath on my skin.

He is right, because I can already feel my soaked panties riding up between my sensitive folds and the way my juices flow for him. When he trails his index finger down the front of my dress, a little squeak erupts from my lips. He cocks his head and then he laughs before he slips his hand up underneath the bottom of my dress. As it rides up, I feel his fingers softly brush my skin and it tickles.

I giggle quietly before his lips devour mine and his fingertip grazes the silky cloth of my panties. When it does, it sends a chill up my spine and pleasure directly to my center. I moan into his mouth as he pushes the cloth aside and I feel his big fingers circle my entrance.

"I fucking want you more than life itself." He growls under his breath after he breaks the kiss hesitantly.

At the same time, I am thinking the exact same thing, but I do not say a word. Instead, I shut my eyes and let him probe me with one finger at first and then he quickly slips in three. Before I know it, I hear the gentle sucking sounds of sex while he is fisting me, and I smell my own brand mixed with sweat.

I swallow hard and look up at him before I ask in a challenge, "Are you going to just fist me? Or are you going to unleash the beast and make me scream for you?"

A naughty smile spreads across his lips before he answers in a deep, gruff voice, "Baby, I am going to make you scream so loud that the whole place will know my name."

No more than a second later, he slips out his fingers slowly as he runs them one last time around my folds in a circle. Then he unzips his pants quickly after he raises his hand to his nose and inhales deeply in approval.

"I need you now." I say quietly so no one hears me besides him.

Then I raise an eyebrow and ask coyly, "By the way, do you like to be called daddy? I may or may not have some unresolved daddy issues to deal with."

As soon as I say it, he smirks before replying in a hushed tone of voice, "Baby girl, if you want me to be your daddy you are going to have to show me what a good girl you are. Usually, I am not into that sort of thing, but for you I will make an exception."

Afterwards, he demands authoritatively, "Now, get down on your knees first so I can see if you are my good girl, and you know how to follow the rules."

When I feel his hand slide up my back and wrap in my hair, I smile because I am going to make him moan in ecstasy as soon as I feel his tip buried in my throat. So, I allow him to lower me down before I open wide, and I devour him whole. As I swallow him deeper, he throws his head back and rolls his eyes before a growl erupts from his mouth. Especially when with one hand I tighten around his balls and squeeze. With the other one, I edge backwards until I feel his entrance and then gently insert my finger one inch.

"Oh, God your mouth feels so warm and inviting. And you know just how I like it. Fuck me." He whispers as he wraps my silken locks around his fingers even tighter now.

When I see him raise his other hand and I feel it brush against my cheek, he runs a finger delicately over my lower lip. His cock instantly reacts as it jerks uncontrollably, and I realize that he is about to shoot his hot load deep within my throat. However, a second later, he pulls him out and then rubs the head on my face until I feel the molten lava spray all over me.

As soon as the last drop leaks out, he stares at me in amusement while he smears it all over on my lips and then he pulls me up for a messy kiss. After he breaks it, he gets that same glint in his eyes again as he turns me around and bends me over the toilet. "Put your hands on the wall baby girl, because daddy is about to christen every hole."

I smile and sigh because I already miss the heat of his cock in my mouth, but I am delighted that he is about to fill my every desire. The only problem is that I can already feel Joanna trying to force her way up to the surface and I am fighting to stay in control because I really like this one. The last thing I want is for her to take over and then have to bury him in the morning.

Chapter 11: Can I Help?

The moment his hands expertly push up my silky red dress, I swallow hard before he smacks my ass with the flat of his hand. When I hear the thin fabric of my silk panties rip before they drop to the floor, I struggle to bend my neck so I can see what he is doing. I smirk before asking in an innocent voice, "Daddy are you going to punish me for being so bad?"

I would have never expected him to do what he does next. Especially, when he grabs me, then he skirts past me before sitting on the toilet seat. He bends me over his knee while I press my palms against the cold metal on the side of the dark green stall. The space is very tight, but when he raises his hand and then smacks my bare ass several times, he makes me whimper in pleasure while his handprint warms my rear end.

I smile as he lifts me up and then helps me stand while I look up into his beautiful eyes. A second later, he states authoritatively in a deeper and darker tone of voice, "Now, bad girl I want to show you just how good you can be. Place your hands on the wall and spread those sexy legs of yours so I can fuck you right. I want to feel just how tight you are for me."

As soon as I obey him, I feel a wet finger rub my rear entrance and then he slides the tip in. I thrust up against his hand suddenly to urge him on as I shut my eyes with a subtle smile on my pouting lips. While desperately hoping that he decides to take me now, I sigh and ask quietly, "Now?"

I look back at him in anticipation as he smiles fully and nods before he spreads my cheeks. He groans as he rubs the tip of his dick on my ass and then lowers it just slightly. As soon as he is poised next to my dripping folds, I hear the door open suddenly. It creaks and then it slams shut before I hear someone walk to the first stall slowly and shut the door before locking it.

We both stay perfectly still as we listen to a steady stream of water hit the toilet basin a second later after the woman unzips her pants. I look up to Jon's face and grimace because I start to feel a cramp in my calf. After swallowing hard, I mouth silently, "I need to stand up, I have a cramp." As the woman flushes the toilet.

When she walks out the door after washing her hands, I feel so relieved but still have this aching need deep inside me. He begins to laugh as he smiles down at me, then he cups my chin with his thumb and forefinger before he devours my mouth and makes a change of plans. While lifting me up, he stares at me intently and then he sits me perfectly on his throbbing penis.

A moment later, I feel the cold metal on my back as he begins to press me up against it with each thrust in. I cry out because it feels so damn good that I don't even realize I am doing it. He glances down at me and raises a hand from my hips before folding it over my mouth and whispering quietly, "Shh."

On the other hand, he continues to dig his fingers into the skin on my hip as he himself can't help but to let out a guttural moan from deep within his chest. As soon as he looks down at me wildly with half hooded eyes, he succumbs to the passion of our love making. Then and only then, does he release my mouth before he leans down and hungrily licks my lower lip slowly. I look up into his eyes again and almost lose myself before I lash out and bite his lower lip.

But when I feel something strange, I know that I am about to cum hard. Harder than even Joanna ever has right before she is about to kill her prey. I am the victor this time finally, because even when she tried to make me let her come out to play, I simply refused to let her have this man. As I stop to wonder exactly why, the orgasm hits me like a thunderous lightning strike.

I close my eyes and moan loudly as he keeps thrusting through it with all his might. And then it comes to me suddenly as I begin to descend from my wonderful high.

"Do I actually care for a man who I have just met? Is there something between us that I can't explain but feel, nonetheless?" I think to myself as he stares deeply into my eyes.

A few minutes later, he explodes deep inside me and shutters uncontrollably. He laughs and then says softly as he lets me down onto my feet afterwards, "Christy, I would love to keep doing this over and over again, but I am afraid our waitress may miss us and then we won't get fed. I don't know about you, but that made me work up more of an appetite than I expected. If I don't eat now, I may eat you up instead."

While ready and willing, I still understand that our bodies need nourishment. By now my stomach is rebelling and telling me that if I do not eat right now, it is going to make me pay for it later. So, I giggle and then state sweetly, "While dining on you is rather wonderful, I still think we need more to eat than each other. That is unless you plan on cooking me for dinner."

He throws his head back as a boisterous laugh explodes from his lips, then he returns his gaze to me and shakes his head with a glimmer in his eyes. When he smiles, I know that everything is alright in my world, and then I watch him zip up his zipper quickly.

As I smooth my dress out, I glance back up at him, and wonder what is so funny. After all, he is just standing there smiling down at me as if there is a private joke that I don't get. He smirks and then leans down to kiss my forehead softly before he asks thoughtfully, "Are you ready?"

I nod, and then he unlocks the door before we return to our table hand in hand with big smiles on our faces. Apparently, no one had noticed our absence and that is just as well when the waitress shows up with our food a moment later.

After a delicious meal, I feel satisfied in more ways than one, but something doesn't feel right, and I don't really know what.

Chapter 12: What Did I Miss?

By the time I wake up the next morning, the sun is already high above my head, so I realize quickly that it is just after 12.

"How in the hell did I get back home? But most importantly, where is Jon?" I ask myself quickly while glancing around the room frantically.

Now more worried than ever, I swallow hard when I smell Jon's Old Spice cologne on me. At first, I could swear that he was here with me, but after I slip out of bed carefully, I can't find him anywhere. And when I hear the neighbors' muffled argument, I yell at the top of my lungs, "Knock it off. You could wake the dead with all that screaming."

"What happened?" I murmur under my breath, because by now I am growing more and more concerned by the minute.

If she did something with him, I would never forgive myself for letting her takeover. More importantly, I was sure that I was under control. So, how did this happen?

While frowning and hunching my shoulders, I suddenly feel my bladder scream at me, so I rush to the bathroom where I relieve myself. When I flush the toilet, I hear something just outside the bathroom door.

"Now what?" I ask myself before I walk over to where I figure that the sound came from and glance down at the floor just outside the bathroom.

I hadn't noticed before this, but because the window is wide-open, a chickadee flew in and is staring up at me with its little black eyes. I watch it curiously and wonder just how I am going to get it back out without harming it. While cocking my head, a thought pops in and I smile sickly.

"Well, why don't you just lean down and snap its neck between your fingers? You can do it. I know you can." Joanna prods sarcastically while she messes with me one last time.

"No! Go away." I exclaim angrily before I slam my fist into the wall next to the bathroom.

"You will not intervene in my normal life anymore. There was a time and a place for you, but I don't need you." I say quickly but then ask quietly in a whisper before I forget, "By the way, did you hurt Jon?"

At first, she does not reply, but as soon as I lean down to pick up the chickadee, she asks loudly, "No, why? Do you care for that man? I have told you time and time again that men are only good for one thing and one thing only." She hesitates for a moment, before adding hatefully, "Don't get your hopes up. He could never love you. No man can. Just remember that when he has another woman bent over a chair and you walk in on them. Don't make me tell you I told you so."

With that in mind, she leaves me for the moment, and I pick up the small bird before it poops on the floor. As I lift it to the window so it can escape, I hear a soft knock on my door. A second later I hear Jon's voice state thoughtfully, "I have lunch. Open up so I can put this down before I spill it."

After I make sure the little bird flies off safely, I shut the window as I yell hesitantly, "Just hold on a minute, I need to get some clothes on."

"Don't do it on my account." He replies sarcastically as I rush to my bedroom for my pink cotton robe with purple hearts all over it from when I was a teenager.

It is at that moment that it all hits me. "Shit!" I exclaim as I smack myself in the forehead with my open palm.

Joanna led him directly to my place. Now surely everyone has seen him and if she ends up killing him at some point, she has doomed the both of us. There is no way that I could ever cover this up and erase the traces of him. Now she has done it and I will be caught up with very soon.

When I stop dead in my tracks, I swallow hard and wonder why. Why of all times would she do this? Of all people? Does she know that I already have feelings for him? Or does she have this deep-seeded need to help me even if she is warning me off? I simply don't get it.

While biting my lower lip, I rush to the door and then stop. I hesitate for a moment as I try to catch my breath, so I don't look too excited to see him. After all, the last thing he needs to know is that I can't wait to see him again alive.

Now that I am sure I can hold my shit together, I sigh deeply before I wrap my fingers around the cold knob and turn it slowly. All the while, in the back of my head, there is still an unanswered question that is bothering me. "Why? Why did she not kill him and then lead him back here of all places?"

As soon as the door opens a crack, I peek out and see his handsome mug before I open it the rest of the way. I can't help but smile, even though I try and fight it because he does not need to know right now how he makes me feel. However, I wonder what his reaction would be if he knew that I am on the border of quite possibly loving him. Would he run the other way, or tell me he feels the same?

Right now, I am just so confused, and I don't know how to handle it. Especially, when I thought that I would never feel like other people do.

"Christy?" he asks with a real sense of urgency as the two coffee cups in his hands look like they are about to spill.

I grab ahold of one just in the nick of time before it slips out of his hand and then I watch as he produces a brown paper bag from the crook of his elbow. He smiles down at me with a glint in his eyes before saying sweetly, "Thank you. I thought I was a goner there for a minute. If you wouldn't have grabbed it, I would have been wearing them in no time flat."

I can't help but laugh at that because he would look so damn cute wearing anything.

Chapter 13: What Is He Doing To Me?

"Don't just stand there. Come sit down at the kitchen table and we can have some lunch." I say absentmindedly as I watch him walk next to me into the kitchen.

"Why does everything about this man have to be complicated?" I think to myself before frowning when I realize that my stomach is growling.

I hear a laugh escape his lips before he places the coffee on the table with the brown paper bag. "I figured after last night that you would be hungry again." He says before smirking with a mischievous glint in his eyes and sliding one of the stools out so he can sit down.

By now, I am looking around frantically to make sure that Joanna hasn't left me any surprises.

"Yes, actually….." I state hesitantly when my eyes land on the note from my aunt.

I skirt past him and then lean up against the counter as I push it out of site. When I turn around, I fake a smile before replying coyly, "I am so glad you could find the place."

He laughs with a twinkle in his eyes and then he states in confusion, "Well, I was just here. It's not too hard to retrace my steps."

Before sighing sadly and looking away, he continues with a confused look upon his handsome face, by saying softly, "You don't remember the incredible night we had last night? Wow. What a way to make a man feel less of one."

After a moment of uneasy silence, I walk over and sit next to him. He glances down at me and half smiles before asking softly, "Would you like a sandwich now? I bought a couple of different ones because I realized that I had absolutely no idea what you liked."

Before answering him seductively, I think up something that Joanna would say to his question and then state smartly, "Well, I would much rather like to suck you dry, but a sandwich would suffice for the moment."

As soon as I say it, he stares into my eyes for a few moments. When I swear that he is about to take me, he smirks and jokes playfully as he states thoughtfully, "You need to eat real food though."

He hesitates before he states sweetly, "I have whole wheat on rye with ham and cheese, or a seafood salad wrap on whole grain pita bread. Which would you prefer?"

I think about it for a minute before I reply softly, "That is so sweet of you. I can't believe you went out and got us lunch. I have never met a man who would have done that for me."

He laughs as he stares at me intently before he murmurs quietly, "Apparently, you have not been around the right kind of men. I always take care of the women I am with."

What he says really starts to eat at my thick husk of a skin and I begin to warm up to the idea of being the woman he is with. But what exactly does he mean by that statement? Are we an item? Surely, we haven't known each other long enough for that. Have we? I have never been in this situation before, because just as soon as any man gets close enough to me, Joanna steps in and slits his throat.

As I swallow hard, my stomach growls once more and I watch him stare at me with that glint in his eyes again. He is more playful than most men and he certainly seems to care what I think, if not how I feel. This is a definite change of pace from the abusive men who only want a quick fuck, and then off with their heads.

"I guess I will have the wrap. I have never tried one before, so this is as good as a time as any." I say sweetly before I bat my eyelashes at him in a half attempt to flirt with him.

Joanna is always so much better at this sort of thing, but if I am to keep Jon around, I need to figure out a way of getting rid of her for good. Of course, this is after I learn a thing or two from her first. In the meantime, I will just have to make sure that Jon doesn't lose some important body parts.

While rolling my eyes, I think about sinking my teeth into the sandwich. Instantly, saliva fills my mouth as I can only imagine the delicious taste of the cheese when it melts. After he hands it to me thoughtfully, I unwrap it carefully as the aroma fills my nose. I glance down at it hungrily before I lift it to my lips and take my first bite.

"Mm. Delicious." I murmur under my breath after chewing it completely and then swallowing as I roll my eyes up while closing my lids.

I sigh softly before I take another bite and then swallow. The delectable tastes of the honey ham, the melted Swiss cheese and the bread all mix to make it practically orgasmic.

"So good!" I exclaim happily before I glance up at him in appreciation.

This is probably one of the few times in my life that trying something new is a good thing.

"I can't tell you how much I appreciate you right now." I say sweetly after finishing off the rest of my sandwich and then taking a big swig of coffee to wash it all down.

While a wicked thought pops in my head a second later, I lower my hand to his inner thigh and trail my fingers slowly in circles up his leg. I wet my lips deliberately when I think about all the things, I could be doing with him. After all, now that my stomach has been filled, I have other needs. Not to mention, I insist on finding out what exactly I had missed out on last night.

I cock my head and look up at him while batting my eyelashes slowly. "I want to thank you for taking such good care of me. Now it is my turn." I say in a flirtatious manner while my fingertips graze over his ever-growing member.

He swallows hard when the last bite of his sandwich sticks in his throat and then he coughs just as I begin to unzip his jeans. While looking down at me with uncertainty, I catch something else in his eyes. Does he want to play?

When he reaches over and brushes the palm of his hand against my cheek on the way to wrapping his fingers in my hair, a squeak escapes my lips. It sounds a bit like a mouse, but he doesn't pay attention. Not when he devours my lips hungrily.

I lace my fingers around his swollen shaft and then pull it out gingerly while his other hand finds my inner thigh so easily. He keeps going up my sensitive skin and discovers that I do not have any other clothes on. One finger traces my already soaked folds and then he slowly slips it in an inch hesitantly. I cry out in need right before someone knocks on the door quickly.

"Fuck!" I yell in frustration when he stops what he was doing and looks down at me with a puzzled look on his face.

"Are you expecting anyone?" He asks quietly so the person at the door can't hear.

Chapter 14: Jon's Issue

I just can't believe the timing of some people. While shaking my head, I glance at Christy briefly before opening the door. After all, the last thing I want to do right now is find out who is on the other side of it. And when I open it fully and see Detective Anderson standing there with a frown on his face, I swallow hard and get ready for the shit show to begin.

"Great." I think to myself as I stare between them in hopes that she does not notice the obvious looks he is giving me.

"Excuse me? May I help you?" I ask hesitantly so it sounds like I do not know him.

I feel her behind me as she wraps her arms around my waist slowly and she uses my body as a barrier between the detective and her. But then she withdraws quickly and steps back when she gets a good look at him. I hear her inhale sharply before she rushes to the security of the bedroom.

As I follow her with my eyes carefully, I hear Detective Anderson clear his throat before stating softly, "I was hoping you could help me out. When you pulled in the parking lot a bit ago, I noticed that you hit my fender. I had hoped that you would try and find the owner. However, when you didn't, I was forced to confront you. Now do you mind if we take this outside so we can get each other's insurance information? I don't think the misses wants me ogling her any more than I want to make her feel uncomfortable."

While I swallow hard, I hesitate and try to figure out what he is getting at. Why call me out here, now? This jeopardizes my whole operation and if she finds out he is a Detective, she will never be able to feel comfortable around me again.

"Sure. No problem. Give me a minute, will you?" I ask hesitantly while wondering what gives?

I roll my eyes at him before I shut the door and walk towards the bedroom to talk to her.

"Christy, baby. I need to take care of something outside. Apparently, I dented this man's fender, and he is not too happy with me because I may or may not have did it. Honestly, the last thing I was paying attention to when I was driving in, was his car as the coffees kept trying to spill all over the leather seat." I say while wincing and trying to lie convincingly.

She nods, and then says quietly, "Sure, no problem. I just want you so bad right now. Please hurry. I may just decide to take care of this itch without you."

The moment she says it, I feel my dick twitch twice to the right and it begins to get even harder as the thought of filling her again fills my mind with delicious memories of last night. When I had spread her wide and filled her in every orifice without complaints, I thought it couldn't get any better, that is until she let me know how much she liked me praising her. So of course, I obliged her repeatedly by filling her ears full of sweetness as I tied her to the bed posts with her stockings and then gave her a rim job excruciatingly slowly before teasing her hole with her play toy.

Trust me, when I say that I was swimming in her juices, I meant it. Not only did I have her begging for mercy, but I had her screaming my name at the top of her lungs. The weird thing is that I felt as if someone else was in control. Because when she talked, she was so much sassier and liked it rougher than she had in the bathroom at the restaurant. Perhaps she just had to relax before she fully trusted me and showed her true colors? However, when I found the skinning knife tucked under her pillow in the middle of the night, I was forced to remind myself that I am sleeping with the enemy, and she is not the love of my life. This is just my job, even if I wouldn't mind filling her tight little ass every night for the rest of my life and then cuddling up behind her so I could get some sleep once and for all. When I leave her for a few minutes, the only thing that keeps running through my head is the fact that I wouldn't mind spending the rest of eternity with her.

"Man, quit thinking with your dick!" I murmur under my breath as I reach the front door.

When I open it and step outside, I look around for Detective Anderson, only to realize that he is waiting for me at the far end of the hall. He waves me to the outside quickly, away from her apartment so he can talk with me. The moment I reach him, he leans in close and asks cautiously, "When the Chief said to get in close, he did not really mean that close. I saw how chummy the two of you have become and I know what that look in your eyes means too. You are getting in too deep, and it is only your first night in her arms. Why don't you excuse yourself for a while and I will keep an eye on that sweet little piece of pussy for you. She is getting under your skin and that spells trouble."

I shake my head and swear under my breath with vehemence, "Son of a bitch. If you even touch a hair on her head, I will fucking kill you. I mean it and yes, I know I am getting too close, but this job calls for it. If I am going to get in thick with her, I need to do this."

He rolls his eyes and hesitates before replying quietly, "Alright, but be careful. Our betters have ended up on the end of her knife and then they disappeared. One of them has gone missing just within the last couple of days, and I figure that she is to blame. So, be careful and watch your back. I just hope you know what you are doing."

A silence hovers between us as I struggle with the realization that I am not fully in control of the situation. I know damn well that if I relax, I may end up in a ditch somewhere or in the woods buried up to my neck in mud. Even worse, she could very easily hack my body up into a million pieces and feed it to the animals.

"Look. I know and I will be always on top of things." I say quietly as I scan the area for anyone who could hear our conversation.

While running my fingers through my hair, I sigh and then state rapidly, "I really need to be getting back before she suspects something. Then I really will be in for it. And yes, I know to contact the Chief as soon as I find out anything."

"Good, I will assure him that everything is fine then." He says before I watch him walk over to the red sports car quickly and he speeds off.

I swallow hard again before I turn around and watch her bedroom curtain move. She had been watching us, and I just hope that she doesn't read lips for my sake. As I walk back in, I feel a real sense of urgency. Especially, when I open the door to her apartment and see her sprawled out across the couch with her vibrator humming away, teasing me.

"Wanna play?" She purrs at me as she slowly slides the tip across her folds and then she runs it up the sleek skin of her belly to her nipples.

She smirks and then sighs as she stares at me and begs for me to join. "Please?" She asks before she turns around and raises her ass up into the air.

"I want to feel that big dick of yours fill my ass and spread me wide." She says seductively as she shakes it for me slowly.

"Mm. Baby you really know how to make a man love you. You are so sweet; I could lick you from head to toe and then repeat over and over again until you couldn't handle it anymore. You're my beautiful baby and I need you so." I say softly with a wicked grin on my face because I know how to make her happy and if I keep it up, she will do anything I want her to.

Chapter 15: Christy, You Are Mine

The moment I hear him state clearly, "Christy, you are mine!" I get giddy and weak in my knees.

Not only have I waited my whole life for a man to say this and mean it, but for some reason the moment it leaves his lips I believe him. Maybe it is because he has me tied up with my ass in the air? Or the fact that he has filled me 5 times in a row without even stopping that has me believing him with every fiber of my being. I don't know why exactly, but I know that he feels the same way about me that I do him. So, this time when he whispers that he loves me sweetly, I close my eyes and choose to believe it for what it is.

Honestly, I have never believed in love at first sight until now, if that is what this is. But more importantly, right now I can't wait for him to slide his dick in my hole so he can make me scream again.

"I guess it is just a good thing that I can't have kids, isn't it?" I hear Joanna whisper from somewhere in the back of my head.

"Stop." I think to myself while I try to push her intrusive thoughts out and pay attention to the way he is making me feel.

"Baby, you are so tight for me. I can't wait to feel your warmth surround me. He states excitedly as I feel his head slide up and down my slit.

While he rubs it over my hole, I inhale sharply with a wicked grin on my lips as I prepare for him to slip it in. But when he stops just at the entrance, he runs his index finger softly up my spine and then down to my hole before he slips a wet finger in and tickles it as he wiggles it in a circle around the rim. I bite down on my lower lip as I clench around his fingertip, then he slips it out and replaces it with the warm, thickness of his head. God, it feels so damn good as he stretches me, and it makes me feel full.

"Fuck!" I exclaim excitedly when he suddenly fills me completely.

With my ass being filled, my pussy begins to throb in need. I beg loudly, "Please, fuck my pussy too. Please."

He smirks as I turn my head so I can see behind me and watch him as he pounds my ass with every thrust. When he digs his fingertips into the skin on my hips, I beg again, "Please."

"Why, of course baby." He replies softly before he pulls him out of my ass and fills my pussy with what I need so badly.

I begin to pant faster as he quickens his pace before he stops suddenly and glances up at my eyes. He exclaims, "I can't hold out much longer." Before he pulls him out and slides him around on my rear.

As he looks around the room, he spots my Pleasure 3000 again and then releases me while he walks over to it. The absence of his touch makes me shiver violently because I haven't realized until just now how warm he makes me feel when he is close to me.

"I know what you want. Who's my beautiful baby?" He asks softly when he runs his fingers over the sensitive skin between my legs.

When I hear him turn it on, I squeal with delight at the thought of filling both holes at once.

"Now, which one?" he murmurs under his breath before rubbing the tip around the rim of my ass and then sliding it in effortlessly.

I moan loudly when he digs his nails into the skin on my hips and thrusts deep inside of my pussy, all the way to his hard, heavy balls.

"Fuck! I will never get over how good you feel Christy." He whispers as he leans over my back and then straightens up to continue his assault of my senses as well as my body.

I cry out again when I feel him pound me hard and fast because I can feel my own orgasm steadily build from deep within. As it hits me, I shake violently and scream out his name in ecstasy, "Jon, I love you."

This time the moment I say it, I see a realization in his eyes. Then as they stare at me half hooded, I see something I have personally never seen before. The look of a man who knows it.

When I shut my eyes, I shiver and watch the fireworks go off under my lids for a few seconds before I hear him grunt and then lose it while filling me.

"Christy." He yells deeply when I feel his hot seed shoot in me, just before he releases his tight grip on my hips.

A few minutes later, I open my eyes to see him staring at me again before he asks hesitantly in almost a whisper while he unties me, "Christy, do you really feel something for me?"

Before I say a word, I pause and think about it seriously because if I blurt out that I am head over heels in love with him, he will think of me as a fool. However, if he feels the same way and I play it down, I may never get him to tell me the truth. So, I close my eyes and hesitate before answering. But when I do, I decide to tell him as I slither away from him and rub my wrists while I sit up against the head of the bed.

"I have never felt this way about any man. Matter of fact, I have never cared at all about anyone before. These feelings are strange for me, and I must be careful because there are things you do not know about me that may make you wish you never found out. I have had a really hard life and that tends to lead to certain things. Things that you might not understand all too well." I say while lowering my voice because I am hoping he won't decide to bolt if he ever learns the real truth.

Chapter 16: Jon's Way

Little does she know that I am playing her, but there is some part of me that really is digging this whole love thing. After all, I have always wanted a woman who would do anything for me. Even if she is insane.

"What exactly are you referring to?" I ask cautiously because this could be the real tide turner.

The Chief would love it if I cracked this case wide open in under a week. Although right now I am enjoying myself too much, so I rather hope that she doesn't spill the beans for the moment. I already know that she has skeletons in her closet, so I say let it be because if she is with me, she is not killing someone and burying the body in an unmarked, shallow grave. That I can handle just as long as I get to fuck her senseless whenever I want to.

"Never mind. It doesn't really matter." She says quickly while I watch her face change subtly.

It is a bit strange when I see this happen. And, in all honesty, it freaks me out a little, but we all have our quirks. What really matters now is the fact that she hasn't killed me yet, even though she always keeps that knife within reaching distance.

As I watch her climb off the bed and stretch, I swallow hard and wonder if she would have told me where her skeletons lie. If so, could I have turned her in after starting to feel something for her besides lust. This is all new to me and I am now wondering if the close proximity to her is messing with my mind just a little. Because how could I care for someone who kills at the drop of a hat? After all, even I have rules I follow.

"I feel filthy. Do you want to take a shower with me?" she asks suggestively while cocking her beautiful face and staring at me with those big, round eyes.

"Mhm. Of course, I do. I wouldn't pass up an opportunity to scrub down my dirty girl." I say perversely while images of her getting fucked against the wall with soap all over her ass fills my brain.

When she offers up her hand and looks up at me with those pleading eyes, I decide that I would follow her anywhere, just as long as I get to be balls deep.

"Baby, you have no idea." I murmur under my breath as I watch that sleek body of hers while my cock is already swelling and readying itself for her.

By the time we get in the shower and turn on the hot water, visions of here spread eagle in front of me plague my thoughts. How did I let myself become obsessed with her? After all, this was just supposed to be another case but has turned out to be so much more. And you know what? If I am not careful, it could bring out my secret past time as well.

"Mm. The hot water feels so good on my sore muscles." She murmurs under her breath as she raises her beautiful face towards the cascading waterfall.

"I agree, baby." I reply while running my hands over her stomach and up to her ample, perky breasts.

Just as I am about to thrust into her from behind, I hear my phone go off. And of course, it is the Chief's secret ring tone.

"Fuck." I murmur under my breath before I kiss her on the forehead and rush out of the shower in a hurry.

As I grab the white, fluffy towel off the rack, I yell over my shoulder to her, "I'm sorry, I must get this. It is work after all. My boss will have my balls if I don't."

"Oh, we can't have that. They are mine and you know that I love sucking on them." She replies sarcastically while she finishes up her shower and I grab the phone right before it would have stopped ringing.

When I hit answer, I hear the Chief's heavy breathing on the other end. "Jon, we need to talk."

"Not now. I am with someone." I whisper into the phone, so she doesn't hear me speak.

As I move into the bedroom and shut the door, I whisper, "I will come in and we can talk in your office. It is safer there."

"Alright, but you are getting in too deep. After all, I don't want to find you missing too in the next few days because you used your little head." He says in a muffled voice as I hear someone else saying something behind him.

He is right. However, I know how to handle myself, even if things go south. I have been trained for exactly these sorts of occasions and that is why I was chosen for this job.

After I hit the end button, I quickly grab my things and get dressed before I hear her open the bedroom door and stand there staring at me. She sighs and then asks sweetly, "Where are you going?"

I lie of course, while I say hesitantly, "I need to go into the office for a few minutes because my boss is having a meltdown. I may or may have not fucked up some paperwork so now I must fix it before he fires me."

She stares at me intensely as if she is trying to figure out if I am telling the truth or not, but in the end, she adds sarcastically, "Don't be too long. After all, I may get bored and decide to find me another man to play with."

I don't doubt at all that she would by the way she looks at me with those big, beautiful eyes of hers and the smirk on her pouty lips.

"By the way, if I am not here when you get back, don't worry because I need to get some things at the store." She says absentmindedly as if she is thinking of something else completely different.

In the back of my head, I begin to wonder if this leaves it wide open for her to go hunting again. Perhaps, me leaving for a while is not such a good idea, but then again if I don't go in, there will be trouble. There always is.

As I open the front door and walk out, I glance back at her and wonder if she will even miss me as much as I will her, so I say hesitantly before I shut the door behind me, "I will be back in a couple of hours. Be here when I get back. Don't make me tell you twice."

    The End

I hope you enjoyed the first book of The Bad Behavior Series called Just Love Me. If you did, then go check out the other two Love Me Now and Love Me Forever.

To my loving husband, mom, sister and all my family that believed in me enough to push me to make this all possible. Thank you. I love you all.

About the Author

M.D. LaBelle is an award-winning, international bestselling author. The genres include anything from children's books to Erotica. She lives in Michigan with her loving husband and four of the six children. Most recently she has started writing on over 200 paid web novel platforms and selling her novels on Amazon, Chapters Indigo, Barnes & Nobles, Kobo, Apple iBooks, Google Play Books and many more. Please feel free to visit her website, Instagram, Twitter and Facebook. Visit M.D. LaBelle's website at

www.mdlabelle.com

Instagram Account

www.instagram.com/M.D.LaBelle/

Twitter Account

www.twitter.com/MDLaBelle1

Facebook Account

www.facebook.com/profile.php?id=100062142582314

I hope you enjoyed reading Just Love Me. Please take the time to read all my other novels if you haven't already. Thank you.

Review it. Please review this novel and let others know what you liked about this book. If you write a review, please send an email to me at m.d.labelle0@gmail.com. Or if you want, please visit me at www.mdlabelle.com

Just Love Me

Book One Of The Bad Behavior Series

Copyright © 2023 M.D. LaBelle

Casper Publishing

All Rights Reserved

This book is a work of fiction. Characters and names are of the author's imagination or are used fictitiously. Any resemblance to an actual person, living or dead, is entirely coincidental.

All rights are reserved. No part of this publication may be reproduced, distributed, or transmitted in any form or by any means, including photocopying, recording, or other electronic or mechanical methods, without the express prior written permission of the publisher, except in the case of brief quotations embodied in critical reviews and certain other noncommercial uses permitted by copyright law. For permission requests, please contact the author through her website: www.mdlabelle.com

www.ingramcontent.com/pod-product-compliance
Lightning Source LLC
LaVergne TN
LVHW061047070526
838201LV00074B/5205